# Sweet

# Ones

by
Len Roberts

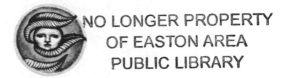

# Sweet Ones

POEMS BY LEN ROBERTS

*len Roberts*

*1/24/00*

MILKWEED EDITIONS

SWEET ONES
Poems by Len Roberts
© 1988 by Len Roberts
All rights reserved.
Printed in the United States of America

91 90 89 88    4 3 2 1

Published by *Milkweed Editions*
Post Office Box 3226
Minneapolis, Minnesota 55403
*Books may be ordered from the address above*

Designed and Illustrated by R.W. Scholes, © 1988

Library of Congress Catalog Card Number: 87-63529
ISBN 0-915943-24-7

The author wishes to thank the editors of the following magazines in which some
of these poems first appeared: *Exquisite Corpse, 5 A.M., The Georgia Review, Green
Mountain Review, Indiana Review, Kansas Quarterly, Memphis State Review, The Mis-
souri Review, New Oregon Review, Northwest Review, Raccoon, Southern Poetry Review,
Tar River Poetry Review, Virginia Quarterly Review of Literature,* and *West Branch.* "Father," #1, under the title "Nights on Olmstead Street," and "Son," #1, under the
title "The Moment," were published by *Poetry.* "A Dish for Each Ticket," "The Driving," and "Building the Barn Door" also appeared in the *Anthology of Magazine Verse
& Yearbook of American Poetry* (Monitor, 1984, 1985, and 1986).

The author also wishes to thank the National Endowment for the Arts and the Pennsylvania Council on the Arts for grants of financial assistance during the years these
poems were written; and, to thank Yaddo for the residencies which gave him peace
and time to write. He is especially indebted to Hayden Carruth and Ken Delahunty
for their continual support and good advice.

Publication of this book is supported in part by grants from The Dayton Hudson
Foundation for Dayton's and Target Stores, The First Bank System Foundation,
the Jerome Foundation, the Metropolitan Regional Arts Council from funds ap-
propriated by the Minnesota State Legislature, with special assistance from the
McKnight Foundation, the Arts Development Fund of United Arts, and by con-
tributions from many generous individuals, corporations, and foundations.

*for Hayden Carruth*

# Contents

## THE DRIVING

## LIGHTING CANDLES IN THE NARROWS

## AT THE TRAIN TRACKS

# I
# *The*
# *Driving*

# Father

for Raymond R. Roberts

1

My father sits in the dark and rocks
his way back to Guadalcanal, to Guam,
cutting his way through canebrake, sipping
rust-water from his rifle's bolt, long-
soaking in the green bathtub brimmed
with ice to break the malarial
fever. Soon he will rise to bury
his brother in water again, so
they won't tear his gold teeth out, but
for now he holds my head against
his chest, the fine hands stretched
across the side of my face, the fingers
kneading gently my cheek bones, my nose,
the valley between my lips and jaw. He
is leaning down to make sure I am still
breathing, saying my name lightly to see
if I sleep. But I do not answer,
just lie there quietly in his bony arms,
knowing how hard it is for him
to set me into the warm bed
and walk silently out of the dark.

## 2

This is the way to stop, my father shouts
as he slams on the brakes and skids
over Lake George ice and poof! slides
into a ten-foot snowdrift. Inside
it's dark, the green dash glowing,
the radio playing Johnny Mathis
while my father whistles and laughs,
clapping my shoulder. What's
the matter, he asks, not fast enough?
and yells for me to hang on as he kicks
in the clutch and throws the stick
into reverse, shouting And this
is the way to start.

## 3

My father has black, I have
red as we sit at the green flaking
picnic table and play checkers, his
hand sure, mine not. Click,
click and swish, jump and king,
he's serious, not letting me win
until he looks into the empty
doorway of the cabin where she is.
Now I hear her moving too,
knocking the pots and pans, clattering
silverware into the yellow
grooves, then silence as she walks
into the bedroom to sit on the white
bedspread and stick pearl-headed
pins into the velvet bag again.
It's your move, I say, but
my father knows that she will soon
put on the imitation pearl
necklace and earrings, hold the black
dress to her body before the silvery
mirror. That by tonight she will
curse the grime of roads on his arms
and hands, the pock-marked holes in his face,
that she will soon scream they should never
have been married as she slams out
the screen door, her face red
and meaty with her other life.

13

4

When the fire alarm went off, my brother
had just begun to tell the elves they'd better
hurry up or Christmas would be late this year, the
cotton beard drooping a good inch from his chin, his pillow
    belly sagging below the wide, black belt.
For a split second even the parents buzzed and
looked around, the lights coming on in their eyes while
we kids filed past them toward the exits, trained
to keep along the wall, not to whisper a word. In the fourth
row my father hadn't left his seat, my mother standing
still beside him in the polka-dot dress, her white scarf
gleaming the hundred feet of chairs between
us. She was holding his hand, and it was plainly awkward, her
standing, ready to leave, him sitting, their fingers half-touching.
I wanted to shout this time it might be real, the flames
already licking their way up from the wood-paneled basement
to the very chair he sat on, that fire any second might burst
onto the wood stage carved with the smiling and frowning
    faces.
I wanted to leave line, disobey the fire rule and run
to his side, pry him from that seat so he could walk
out like everyone else, before the entire building
came blazing down.

5

Breath gone, eyes so rheumy
he couldn't tell the suit, my father
lifted each card to my face for me to say
spade, club, diamond, heart, watch
his long fingers set them on edge. Corners
first, sides, then the roofs, extending
room by room until they covered
the entire table and he'd start
stacking the cards on top, the second and third
stories, the fourth and fifth, his hand
no longer shaking, not one tremble.
Some nights, when he drank more, he brought
out the rubber men, women and children, the metal
cars, stuck matches into bits of sponge
and lit them as streetlights
in the strange town of cards. Vroom,
vroom, he whispered after clicking
off the kitchen light, his face nearly
flat on the table as he pushed the cars
in and out of one-stall garages, lifted
a man into a side room he said was a bar,
asking, Can't you hear that music?
Nights, now, I wake in the dark and swear
I hear laughter, a tune I can never
quite make out, and then him talking
the way he did about nothing,
about silence, the empty space between walls and ceiling,
lifting the cards, adding on until he reached the end
and handed me the last one to set on top.

# The Driving

When she got to Cook's Taxi Stand, the yellow
light shone from the window onto snow
piled three feet deep by the curb,
and she suddenly realized it was twenty below,
that she'd been standing there for minutes in her bathrobe.
Slowly, as she knew where she was, she also
remembered where she had come from, the small flat
rising in her memory like a dead fish, unexpectedly,
to the surface of a lake. She thought
of the two boys in their pajamas, the pock-marked
man still sitting at the white table.
She wondered if she had cancer. They had
had a fight, she remembered sticking him in the stomach
with a butcher knife. My God, she muttered
just as an old couple walked by, the woman
staring, the man looking into the yellow window
where Mr. Cook sat at his table.
And where could I go, she asked the parking
meters as she started home, the snow
no longer pricking when it touched her slippered
feet, the snow feeling good, cold like that
until she thought about lying down in it, there
on Remsen Street, letting them find her there,
letting them see what she had been driven to.

# Shoveling Snow in Cohoes, New York

First the barbershop, then Irene's Beauty Salon,
then up Ontario Avenue to the Hill and houses
with wreaths and small bells ringing
on the doors. Out there I walked
slowly, the ear muffs and falling snow
buffering the clanking chains of cars and trucks,
dogs barking as though in silent movies
from their drifted back yards.
When the old man and woman passed by in their long coats and
    scarves,
I was happy not to hear a word they said, just
watching their breaths rise into the pearl sky
that streaked with sun.
I was glad not to hear the kids screaming across the street,
glad not to hear the small avalanche toppling
from the low branch of the pine tree just before me.
Back there my parents would be shouting while
the record player blared Jimmy Dorsey, but
I did not have to hear them, out in the snow falling
faster than I could shovel, not once thinking
I had to go back, I had to listen.

# Sleighing down the Clay Hill

Rudy goes first, then Porky, and I
follow, knowing they're ahead of me in the gulley
of the Clay Hill only by the swishing
and stray thumps of sleds on frozen snow.
I'm afraid of the boulder somewhere ahead, and
of Bill Bowen flying behind, but it's all
I can do to swerve away from the rocks and bushes
that keep leaping up. The sled rises higher
at one curve, then floats so I can see the gulley's
ridge, and then over to the street light gleaming
near the American Bowling Alley, the entire city
glimpsed for a split-second as though lit
by lightning, the silent cars drifting ghost-like
down Ontario Avenue, the yellow circle of the town
hall's clock. I want to stay there, suspended, free
of the terror of not remembering which curve leads
to that boulder, but as soon as I think it I'm yanked
down to the sliced white tracks of those who have gone
before me, my stomach landing first, then chest, thighs
hitting, hands wrapping around the steering
paddles, trying to put that one glimpse of the quiet,
larger world out of my mind, trying to call back the warning
signs, the flap of a refrigerator's discarded
cardboard box, the battered ash can zipping before my eyes
like frames in a movie run mistakenly at high speed, each
one popping up and as quickly disappearing, until I
remember exactly where the boulder is, sure again
that I will miss it, that I will keep on missing it.

19

# The Odds

I woke last night with mucus
in my throat and thought of Dorothy Blake,
the blue thermos she unscrewed
on her desk behind me in eighth grade,
how she drew the long line of phlegm
from her rotting lungs, oozed
it into the open bottle. Each time
she squeaked Oh no, I was the only one
to hear, always ducking my head just
as the clouded numbers on the blackboard
disappeared in the stench of whatever
she had eaten that morning. She'd
be dead in a year, our teacher told us
when Dorothy had gone again to the nurse's
office, and then added that five of every
twenty-five kids our age would not live
to be adults. We looked around at each other,
some not believing, others hoping
it would be Al Aubon, or Jackie Foster,
some wishing Louise with the bad mouth
or snotty Ann would be the first to go, but
then Dorothy walked back in, her long
bones gleaming beneath her chalk-
white skin, her blue eyes watery
with what was coming, polka dots of blood
already dry on her green silk blouse.

# Sunday Morning Sink Bath

It took her hours in the kitchen
to remember how afraid she was
to walk to the dark church, agreeing
at six to attend the eight o'clock
mass, but then changing her mind because
her dress was never pressed neatly enough,
strands of hair always fell into her eyes.
All white she stood, deciding
at the sink, her large stomach and thighs
pale as the porcelain, her skin blue-shadowed,
so she seemed covered with barely visible
bruises that she rubbed the wash cloth in circles
over and over, as though she were scrubbing
entire years from her life. And when
she was done, how lovely she was, bending
to button my crisp, white shirt, to tighten
the tie that was always too short, pressing
the dime into my palm just before
she reached for the door.

# Ushering in the New Year
# at the Cohoes Theater

For the thirty-seventh time I watched
Yuri pick potatoes among the billowing
wildflowers, I saw Lara in a devil-red
dress drinking brandy with an old, nearly bald
man, and I let Donna, the twelve-year-old from St. John's
Alley, crawl from seat to seat in the front left
corner of the theater, unzip the boys' pants and suck
cocks for a dollar a head. I didn't flash the light
on the couple who came in every Saturday night to sit
in the one seat at the back on the right, her dark
coat or his tan coat over them both like a blanket,
only strangers ignorant enough to sit beside them.
Instead of walking down the carpeted aisles,
I stood in the back eating popcorn, breaking
the theater usher's law, thinking about Mary,
who would be waiting for me in two hours to lock
the doors so we could ride to River Road. But
I couldn't stand there very long thinking about
her tight green dress, for here was Lara's mother
thrashing on the bed, her red hair sexual, her ass
gleaming, and there was Denise, the candy counter
girl, aglow, and Patty, her smiling friend
who counted out change slowly into hands
that flashed brief seconds on top of the fluorescent
glass before they faded back into the dark.

# Pine Lake, 1958

"Jailhouse Rock" and "Don't You Step
on My Blue Suede Shoes" filled
the pine-walled, pine-floored
pavilion at Pine Lake where my older brother
and Bev, his new girlfriend, shimmy shimmy
coco-bopped and strolled their way out
the double doors. An hour
later he walked back in with
dark wings on the crotch of his khaki
pants and everyone laughed. He laughed
too, standing there in the shiny light, fifteen,
then turned to jerk and sling his hips
like Elvis, grind his gleaming black shoes
into the circles of sawdust, as though he wanted to
drill holes clean through the floor.

# Blacktop

After I had pushed and shoved a barrow filled and refilled
with four hundred boiling pounds of blacktop
for thirteen hours, Old Leo came up to me and winked,
said there was a man down the block who would pay
fifty bucks, so how about one small job?
It was dusk, the hose water cold again
as I followed him down the walk to where the
concrete had heaved and cracked, where we pickaxed
and shoveled and hauled until the blacktop was
finally poured and leveled. Eighty-two
and the man still wasn't tired, not even leaning
on the rake as he watched with those turtle
eyes, ready to catch the slightest mistake,
watching me watch him back, him smiling, wiping
tobacco juice from a stubbled chin, telling me I had
a long life ahead, now go get more blacktop.

# The Breadman

One of my silent nightmares has Marjorie
walk away with another man, and I can only sit
at the white table drinking my glass of beer.
I have no proof she's unfaithful
but when the phone rings and I answer it
to a click, I add one more thought, like
the beads at the poolroom when I drop a ball in.
It's like this—on the bread route
the long drifts of snow bind me in
to some wind-driven shack at the end
of a road no sane man would deliver
on, and the woman's a little fat, and not
much talk, but I can never pass
it up when she stands in the doorway, the bathrobe
open down to the bra, or when she turns
and says There's coffee brewing,
her words thick, warm, the below-zero
at my back sure to be there when I come out.
I know it's not right, and I pay with my sleep,
night after night twisting the sheets,
hearing Marjorie snore on her side of the bed,
deep in herself, not one twitch.

# Another Spring on Olmstead Street

She's out there again with her five-cent
packets of seeds for green beans and beets,
the small tomato plants humped in green cardboard
containers, on her left a box of sifted
soil, on her right the brown beer bottle.
Elvis sings "Love Me Tender" from the open
window as she scoops the soft roots
in the palm of her hand before setting them in.
A dog barks, a car rattles down the alley
but she is gone so completely
into the stems and leaves that not one of us
watching from the house dares to go out
and touch her bare shoulder, not one of us
calls her name into the beginning dark
where she dreams and digs, where she buries
time and again her white, white hands.

# My Father's Cough

My father coughs again, hawkers
phlegm into the blue hankie, gets up to spit
more out the door after looking up and down
the block to be sure neighbors aren't
on their front porches. When he comes
back in, he asks if I want to count
coins and then unclasps the leather
breadman's purse to shimmer change
onto the table. Pennies, nickels,
dimes and quarters, the rare half-
dollars, stack after stack, while
he drinks and hacks, until
I cough too, put my hand over my mouth
the way he does, making him jump
from his seat to whirl me
a split-second against flowers growing
on the tin ceiling before I fall
back into his bony hands.

# A Dish for Each Ticket

In those soft summer hours between seven
and dark, when the loudest noises
were the screen doors slamming or
the watery mutterings of neighbors floating
over the backyard fences, then she
would scream that he didn't make enough,
the fish cakes were burnt, she
couldn't live in a hole like a pig without
a nickel. Quickly he'd unsnap
the breadman's leather purse, place
the change in her hands and say, Go
to the movies. It was the only time
my brother and I went anywhere alone
with her, knowing she was happy to have us
because each of our tickets bought another
brown cup or saucer, because in the dark
we'd finally disappear and leave her feeling
cool, rich, eating buttered popcorn with
three heavy dishes nestled in her lap.

# II
# *Lighting Candles*
# *In The Narrows*

# Lighting Candles in the Narrows

for Hayden Carruth

I light four candles in a circle
around me to keep away the mosquitoes
who know I am the only human on this
narrow island, and I think in the silence

of the early Sunday mornings I floated
in cassock and surplice behind the stone
angels of the altar, stole sips of Christ's
blood from the thick glass tumbler, witnessed

the white circle of His Body rise. It
might have been all right if Father hadn't tried
to kiss me in the sacristy, if my
brother hadn't lost his mind in the air

over Okinawa while parachuting for his country.
Immediately a list of injuries appears,
from the worst to the least, more
than five, more than ten, and I know it will grow

longer and longer, and that nothing will stop
it. Certainly these four floating candles cannot,
just as those other candles could not,
always a shock to see them there, still, in the mind's

dark, three on each side of the altar, each one
higher than the last, peaked toward the center,
and my body stretched up to light them,
trembling, not with hope, nor memory, nor

sorrow, just trying to hold steady
long enough to place the flame directly
on the wick, which always hissed
that split second it lit.

# Making Sure the House Is Locked

The school bus stops but no one gets off
and I think of my son lying in the hospital,
tubes in his nose and throat, needles in his arms,
his head in darkness for two days, on the verge.
I pick up his basketball and sponge
football, the playboy puzzle I gave
as a joke, which he put together within
the hour. I pull back the curtains
and wrap the ties evenly around them, raise
the blinds to let the sun in. It was a mistake
coming back here to his silence, feeding
the cats, making sure the doors are locked.
Walking out the back door I find his baseball bat
in the too-high grass, pick it up
and for a moment think of going back
into the house to tell him it's time for cutting.
Some day, I hear myself say, he will be here
again, the bruise of his face clear, his
left eye even with the right, his leg mended,
the thirty-seven stitches in his forehead closed.
In no time at all, I say, closing the door
tightly, testing it, turning the handle with care,
hoping insanely such a small act might save him.

# Building The Barn Door

for Doreen

It is snowing, and your brother,
back from a foreign war, has come
to help build the new sliding barn door.

Wrapped in parkas you two first square
the frame, 16 by 16, then nail
the cross brace. Hammering the spruce

boards you think this time he's all right,
not a single nail bends under his blows,
his mouth open with words, not screams.

Duck-walking down the opposite side
he says he's been off the thorazine
for months, the clear white snow shining

in his eyes. The wind down the hill plummets
below zero, but he won't go in until he bolts
the 2 by 6, the galvanized guide and runner,

until the door rises to cover the dark
mouth of the barn. He won't even look
at the light in the house, the chimney's

smoke, until the handle's on, the padlock,
the rectangle of rubber cut and tacked.
Even as you say your feet are numb,

the wind's driving water from your eyes,
he stomps through the crusted snow, bends
to bevel the door's edge for the tightest fit.

# The Black Hammer

Fog fills the small yard ringed with roses
as I sit at the white table sipping coffee,
hearing the ocean's waves somewhere
out there in that gray, a few
gulls crazed enough to fly in this weather.
Suddenly I remember my father sat like this
at another white table, sipping Schaefer's
from brown bottles, that I raise my hand
with the same doubts, as though any second
the black hammer that drove him might now
drive me into the ground.

# The Block

Last night I listened to a man shovel
the sidewalk while the snow continued
to fall, the rumble of the blade
as it hit rough spots, the swish
when it slid across smooth concrete, the quick
chop of the pick for the ice underneath,
and I remembered those five a.m.'s when
my father rose to shovel the entire block, his
father coming out quickly to join him, their two
backs bent for an hour before work. I was ten,
spying from our second-story window, and did not know
then how they felt out there in below-zero morning
that was just starting to crack, pearl-like,
with the sun slowly rising over Cohoes Carrybag Factory.
I did not understand their stopping to look around
   as though someone had called, their
smiling at more snow falling, working back to back
from the center of the block, moving further and further
apart until they reached the ends of the walk and then,
without one word, without even a wave of the hand, entered
   their separate doors.

# Making Galumpkis

My grandmother pounds sausage and rice
into small mounds, then unrolls the cabbage
leaves to drown them in the long blue pot brimmed
with tomato sauce. I help her wrap what
we call galumpkis, then watch
her shove the pan into the oven, straighten
to whisper her cooking prayer to the white cross
above the table. While they bake she repeats
the story of my father out in ten degrees
below zero, drinking whiskey with that woman,
my mother, says when they sent him home
from the war he weighed only ninety pounds
and had to lay in bed for a year. In the pantry
she mutters malaria, Marjorie, jungle rot
to the dark pots and pans, then turns,
her voice rising as she clatters the plates
and cup down, tells me to eat. So I do, gulping
five of them at the first serving, unbuckling
my belt in my grandmother's honor, while
behind me she kneels and clicks the beads
of her rosary, rises only to see
if I need more, then taps once, twice, three
times on my forehead, looks me right in the eye
to ask if I'm still behaving.

# The Trains
for Walt

This morning my friend called to say it's a struggle
trying to keep the thirty degrees below zero out
of his house, but I thought of his father
in Scranton winter, on the hill with no trees,
of his sister who stopped eating because the man
she loved had a fatal stroke. Now he invites me and
my family over to see his basement again, full of train
tracks, six complete lines with cars, cabs, cabooses, white
churches with spires, post offices named with towns, great
spreading yellow maples, silver birches, sidewalks, half-inch
panes of glass in the candy store window. Small
rubber women, children and men stand on platforms
or walk down back alleys about to pet a dog, to lean
on a fence and talk to a neighbor. At times the sky
darkens on a green hill, a woman falls off
the earth and is lost in the carpet. Names
and addresses flourish in miniature official records books,
a child goes into the new hospital and does not come out.
Five old men meet every morning until there are four.
A girl walks from the church knowing she's married
too young. At night the dark is complete except
for the red and green traffic controls and thin beams
of the engines' headlights, the old Lackawanna
steaming in cold blown from the Lake, the Reading
rolling like an unstoppable wave to the swoosh
and whirr of wheels on steel drifting over bypasses,
bridges, through tunnels leading only from dark to dark.

# Rising for the Milk Route

While the milk truck idled on the cobblestones
Nick kept whispering Bunny's name, his sweetheart, and
Jeannine's, his kissing girl, and Diane's, the smart
one who lived in the brick house on the hill
where he could never touch her. In two
years he would be sent home from Okinawa swallowing
benzedrine and thorazine, his mind reassembled
by thirty-five electric shocks, but in the dark
kitchen he hummed, slicking back the wave
of hair shining with vaseline, slowly slipping
on the gold chain and cross, the gold ring
with a black onyx and diamond chip, the initial
N glittering in fancy script. "I found my thrill"
and "Don't you step on my blue suede shoes"
he sang as he watched himself in the mirror,
turning only to sip steaming coffee from the blue
cup or to erupt into a quick jitterbug
with his invisible partner.

# Nick's Unborn

Last night Nick heard the snow seethe
in the weeds and ghost trees, and he
wondered about the twins miscarried
years ago in the night of a great snow
storm. Did they still hover around their mother
as his friend said they would, until
the right words were said? In zero
degrees he imagined their unformed bodies,
milk-white, freezing, their lumps of eyes,
the inch-long arms and legs, and he gave
them names, so many names he could hardly say
them as fast as they rushed into his head,
Anthony, David, Mary, Helen,
each name a puff of breath into the cold
dark where it ascended before
it was completely gone. "The meek shall
inherit the earth," Sister Sylvia had said
so many years ago, and her words rang
in Nick's head, as though they had something
to do with the two deaths, but Nick couldn't
figure what, so he bent and snapped off
an ice-sheathed stalk of golden rod and put
it into his mouth, cracked it carefully, tongued
the ice, and spat the weed out
before he walked back toward the house.

# Coal Miners

I wake from a dream of coal miners
in Cohoes turning into glittering pieces
of coal, burning, hands and faces on fire, and
in this north light of a cold room I shiver, feel
the wind move through me as it blows into
their ashes; I know we are in this together.

No wonder I don't care the day is breaking
in half while I can still see the copper light
in the coal tunnel of dream, the miners' bodies
burning in the dark seams, and I think
this is not hell, but heaven, light
arms and chests, translucent hands
and sapphire necks, each one touching
off the other until there is nothing left.

## MY UNCLE CHAUNCEY DROVE MY AUNT ELEANOR

over two-hundred miles every day because
she had Alzheimer's, couldn't remember
where she was, where she had been, and
had to see the elephants in the zoo again,
stop in to see her friend Rose
for the third day in a row. When
they left the house he had his teeth
clenched deep in his jaw, she
was smiling, sixteen again, bowing
to swoop up the tall-stemmed tulips,
oooing and aaahing as she looked into
the yellow and red, ripping the petals
off in puffs of circus colors just
before she skipped the rest of the way
down the walk. Sometimes she'd call
him Pete or William, or some other
man's name, and hold his hand a way
she had never held his hand, and
Chauncey would get jealous although
he was sixty-two and knew her mind
was riddled with time like the rotten
oak log in his back yard the carpenter
ants had eaten their way through. Holding
the car door for her to slide in, he'd shout,
Who's Bill, and who in hell are Merrill
and Ray, What in hell have you
been doing all these years, but she'd
just bend over to ask in the low, sweet voice
that had so recently come back, if he would
please peel out the way he used to, leave smouldering
tracks by the yellow curb in front of their house.

# The White Towel

Last night the man turned off
the Northway, returning to the small
town the back way, past the Falls
where he and a girl whose birthday
he still remembered stripped to swim
in the Number Eight Hole.
He tried again to see the subtle blend
of brown and green in her eyes, he lifted
his hand from the steering wheel
to feel the heaviness of her breast.
His wife beside him said nothing, but the boy
in back asked what he was doing with his hand
and the man replied Nothing. And
it was nothing, he thought—the wet hair,
his fingers stuck in it, the towel white enough
to guide them, after their swim, back.

# Pretending in Paestum

All I remember is the worn, packed sand
the Italians called ground, weeds growing
tall as a boy through cracks in the blocked
stone seats, the white heat
of the sun firing our bodies, our breathing.
I stood where the lions had entered,
you stood in the center, and we timed
how long it would take me, four days starving,
whipped and caged, now pricked with spears,
to roam the arena's walls, how long
to circle you once, twice, three,
four times, each circle smaller, each
time the smell of your body stronger,
your arms and legs burning for what we took
to be the last time, your eyes now
close to my eyes, disbelieving,
knowing so well my betrayal.

# Letting Go

On the red picnic table a quart of tea
sweetens in the sun, a disc of lemon
gleams like a raft on top, and I imagine
we are lying there, on that yellow, the brown
sea perfectly still, no clouds in the sky,
only the scrub pine's needles above us whispering
Let go, Let go, as one, then another, and another
comes undone from the branch to fall
like bodies all about us.

# Cutting down the Wood Shed

Starting to cut down the old shed attached to the barn, first
  the corner posts chainsawed, then working my way to the
  center,
all the while thinking about my sixteen-year-dead father
  sleeping entire weeks on Boney's Bar, waking
only to eat steak sandwiches or piss or buy drinks for the house.
I remember him coming home in 8 p.m. summer evenings hot and
  dusty from peddling his cakes and doughnuts and seven kinds
  of bread,
how he didn't have a good tree like this old oak to lean his
  back against,
how he sat in the sauna-tenement flat lifting those fabulous
  gold glasses of beer
while sweat rolled down in beads from both of them.
As sweat beads roll all over me standing here in the shadow
  of the chainsaw's blue exhaust and roar,
half of me afraid it will kick back to my arm or my face if
  the blade hits a nail that's been waiting inside for years,
the other half rigid, muscle hard as it can be, determined to
  cut my way through this iron-seasoned wood until the entire
  structure comes crashing down.

# Shoveling Snow

For two days the snow has not stopped
falling, thick and wet, just last night
dropping an entire foot, making me go out
again at six a.m. with the shovel. First
the porch, then the walk, lifting the cakes
of snow, always the same, as though
I, or the snow, were no different
from when I shoveled it years ago.
The very thought makes me shiver more
than the zero-degree wind blasting down
the hill, more than the flakes that
inadvertently slip down my neck. Imagine
coming back again and again like this,
I mutter, but then hear my wife tap
at the window, her blue sweater
with pink stars buttoned up for warmth,
and she's waving me in, time for breakfast. The
gray is beginning in her hair too, her body
softening like mine, and for a second
I think of finding her dead some morning
like this, or her finding me, an inescapable
fact. Then she taps again, twice,
making me turn toward the door—
but I do not want to go in, not yet,
for how can I say a word, any word, that
will make sense as she flops pancakes
onto my plate and, smiling, pours
steaming coffee into the heavy white cup.

# III
# *At The*
# *Train Tracks*

# At the Train Tracks

Another springtime, another dollar. I wonder
as I drive from one job to another
how many more hours, honest-to-God alive
hours I have left, how many more Christmasses
I will buy the unnecessary gifts, how many more
summers limit myself to two weeks vacation on a lake
when that's all I'd like to do with my life.
Held up at the tracks I watch the B & O line,
the L & N, the Lackawanna, the Reading, the rusted metal
wheels clickety-clacking like mad days
on the shining steel while behind me automobiles
pile up, one driver blowing his horn
as though there were some other way across.

# Pregnant, She Dances

The storm had stopped, leaving the ocean
calm, the roses dripping near where
you stripped off the white blouse and white shorts
to stand completely white in the knee-high grass.
Arms held over your head you danced beneath
oranges, beneath clouds, not knowing
I watched from the window, your feet
kicking sand ankle high, your pregnant belly
floating out, stretching your skin like a bubble
in batter, the roundness of it rising and rising,
as though each leap created the child more fully,
as though each sudden escape from the earth gave it more life.

# Son

for Joshua L. Roberts

## 1

Walking the three tiers in first light, out
here so my two-year-old son won't wake the house,
I watch him pull and strip ragweed, chickory, yarrow,
so many other weeds and wildflowers
I don't know the names for, saying Big, and Mine,
and Joshua—words, words, words. Then
it is the moment, that split-second
when he takes my hand, gives it a tug,
and I feel his entire body-weight, his whole
heart-weight, pulling me toward
the gleaming flowers and weeds he loves.
That moment which is eternal and is gone in a second,
when he yanks me out of myself like some sleeper
from his dead-dream sleep into the blues and whites
and yellows I must bend down to see clearly, into the faultless
flesh of his soft hands, into his new brown eyes,
the miracle of him, and of the earth itself,
where he lives among the glitterings, and takes me.

## 2

Last night I brought in more
split oak, five loads, enough
to outlast the coming snow, and
my son, about as long as one
of the logs, insisted he carry
a bark scrap, a branch or stick in too.
By the back door's light he stood
while I loaded my arms with as much
as I could, watching shadow cover
half his body, light on the other
half that faced up the hill, toward
the skeletal trees that seemed to
wave at him while he waited, patient
in the cold, for his father to go in.

### 3

It's cold out here, the worst time
of the year, twenty below and snow
dropping brittle as ice, and still
he follows me up the hill to
the stone row, and over, into the sudden
silence of evergreens. To every question
I ask, he says Tine, which means Fine,
he's fine, no matter how cold his father's toes
get, no matter where the wind snaps my eyes,
he's truly warm, wrapped in the puffed air
of his snowsuit, the black boots shining
into the deep drifts of snow.
Tine, tine, tine, he repeats to the cardinal
flying cockeyed in the snow-sky, to the pine cone
he finally manages to pick up in his fumbling
mittens. And he is! I shout,
not caring if my neighbor's dogs bark berserk
from the echoing down into the barn and across
the road into their house, not caring if my wife
comes to the back door, all the way, a good half-mile
down there, to look up to these woods where I skip
and romp, beside my child, beside myself.

4

When I open the desk drawer, I find two
teaspoons and a green plastic soldier, his arm
up, waving invisible others ahead, and in my shoes
the paper clips, the wax balls I use
to plug my nights with, a battery
he's removed as stealthily as any thief
from the flashlight left foolishly
on the kitchen chair. He even sneaks
across the cold pine floor of January
to tuck what is precious into the soft
holes between the sofa's cushions, making slight
lumps under the rugs. From the window he looks
at the moon as though it is his, then
toddles from the living room
to find the dark pantry again, the red
enameled pots and pans hung by wooden handles, his head
bent so the world won't see him, especially
this father who goes down on his hands and knees
among the bags of sugar and cans of soup, who growls,
sniffs into the three corners where he is
not, then turns back toward the kitchen
light, leaving the door ajar behind him.

He lifts the dead bee to the window light and
yells Die, Die, his new word, then looks at me to confirm
he's got it right. Before I can nod
he's torn a wing off, a leg, poked a pencil
tip into its belly, then let it drop among
his scattered toys. Just a month ago
he could hardly walk, but now he's crashing out
the screen door after a fly, he's picking up maple
branches carefully, shouting Nake, Nake
because he can't say his s's yet. Soon
he'll be down by the pond to toss
rocks at the frogs, he'll be on
his hands and knees searching through the unmown
grass for that special stone. Even as the light
fades and I wave from the porch, he teeters
after robins stick-stepping across the lawn,
follows fireflies into the stone row's brush
where they slowly float up into the darkening
branches of the oak.

6

My son walks to the third tier, turns
and yells for me to Come on, and be quick
about it, I think, before the Farewell to Summer
crumple completely in his hands, gifts
he intends to bring back to his mother
from our morning walk. The straw
flies apart when he touches it,
the thistles prick, but still he bends to sniff
each flower he finds, he yanks them up.
When he sees the moon fading in the west
he shouts and runs across the timothy
field to where it grows above the trees.
At the stone row he can only stop and look.
Then he wants the red leaves of the poison oak,
the long, thorned stem of a wild rose. He won't
turn back to the white house even though
his hands are full, begins instead to walk up South
Hill, where he knows there are flowers he hasn't seen yet,
Sweet ones, he says, blue and red and gold and green.

# Death Planes

All night they hovered above us, the Mustang
and Grumman Avenger, Hellcat, Flying Fortress
with glass swiveling turrets, small men inside firing
machine guns with bullets winding in on long curls
of belts, and I wondered why in hell I'd put those death
planes above my three-year-old's bed, the greens and blacks
and reds and blues and yellows bobbing and swerving as
they rotated in endless revolutions, illusionary
rainbow, illusionary beauty. And I was glad my father
never put anything in my room except his dark body
those nights he'd come to sit on the edge
of my bed, my world then, everything beyond it unsafe,
fearful, especially the black below where the devil waited
with his spiny red claw, where the cliff grew and grew
that I fell from every night in nightmare. He sat
there in outline of light and sang some song he'd brought back
    from the bar or told stories. . . .
But no. What he did most was exist so much in the darkness
    of himself
that I felt it flow out of his body and into my body,
blackness that became, as I grew older, my core,
so I found it waiting nights outside the window, or
    in the funeral parlor's flowers blooming,
in the slow steps of old men, the rooms of those I love just
    before they die. I tell you
that blackness seeped out like sap, thick and luxuriant,
into my eyes and forming hands and cock and brain and
    strong back
that I might enter the world of sunlight and automobiles
and blazing red scarves without him.

# Talking on the Telephone

Thirty years later I try to remember
the telephone number back on Olmstead Street,
see the black base and speaker I took
into the cold hallway those long winter
nights I talked to all the girls
I loved. Inside the warm kitchen
my mother and father whispered,
now and then the click of dishes
set into the sink, the pop
as the top snapped off another Schaefer's
bottle, but out there it was wind
drafting under the front door, finding
its way up the stairs to where I would sleep,
wind coming in from the back, too, down
the long corridor with its one dim light.
Hello Mary, hello Suzanne, Dee Dee
with the blue angora sweater, how are you
tonight, I wish you were here, and then
the Drifters started to sing "Save
the Last Dance for Me," my feet
propped against the dark wallpaper,
my nose and hands chilled, becoming numb
while their voices flowed into my warm ear.

# On Agnes Island

The lake has changed this past
hour to treacherous again, the way
it so often does, waves pounding
the rocks where we sit on lawn chairs,
jackets pulled up about our necks,
staring at the moon and stars. So many
have looked at this, you say, and
there is in your voice the sadness
of the waves and moonlight as
it glimmers and fades. In the tent
behind us Joshua stirs, screams
once in terror at what the night
has brought into his sleeping.
Then complete silence for four
or five seconds before the wind
comes again, stronger than before,
knocking pine cones down from limbs
we did not know shook above us.

# Edisto Island

The ocean keeps sending in waves, one of every
five or six bringing a message—this one says Get out,
that one Come back, another has a seventeen-year-old
girl with brown hair riding deep in its green, another
my grandmother waving the last time I saw her, heavy legs
   propped on the empty crate that used to hold oranges.
My son wants to build castles so I make mounds
with his animal pail, and he kicks them down, wildly laughing.
My wife reads GOURMET, planning the meals
we will eat, the thick sauces, spices, holding
up a page of strawberry dessert, a page of lemon meringue
   with an English castle behind it.
I wonder what the castle has to do with the meringue
but then five pelicans fly by in a line and I think
of my brother losing his mind while parachuting over Okinawa.
Then my father's face, a lover's, a grade school teacher's
drift by and I nod to each, a quick hello-goodbye wave of hand
before I go back to fingering shells, searching for sharks' teeth
that gleam blackly from thousands of years tossing
   in the wild sea.

# Polishing the Work Boots

First the stiff bristle brush to
clean out the dried sticks and caked mud,
then digging into the thin can
of saddle soap, melting it between
my fingers, then onto leather.
Toe, sides, tongue beneath the laces, heel,
wedging the paste where the sole meets
the upper shoe, warm and long drawn-
out circles, small, then larger, then
small again, thinking of the wood
waiting to be split on the third tier,
surprised by the yellow and white chrysanthemums
Nancy found and set on the table
although this is December Pennsylvania,
finally stopping to pick up the clean
white cloth to wipe the excess off,
snapping the rag, for the hell
of it, into the night.

# The Bank Barn's Tilt

Over three feet of snow in two
days and the guy who plows my driveway
bedded with flu, a slit in my green boots
and still I'm here under the maple,
shoveling the walk. When I straighten
my back to take the ache
out, I see the crazy angle the barn
has tilted into the past
hundred years, tell myself again that
someday
I will climb to bolt the steel
cables and winch the sides plumb, remembering
my friend's story of the farmer down
the road who tried that, but the cable
snapped and knocked him thirty feet
into death. Death, death, death,
that's all I think about, the fathers
ahead of me, one by one, going down,
the fathers behind me, rising, as
though I'm on an escalator and there's
no way off. And there isn't, the snow
seems to say by falling faster, thicker,
filming the walk again, the wind knocking
icicles off the gutter, making me duck, hunch
my shoulders until they stop dropping
and I can look up, see one about two feet
long stuck in the bank beside me, dazzling
the blank white with prism pinks and blues
   and yellows.

# The Killing

I try to sleep in my son's
bed, the bears and rabbits and chipmunks
cartwheeling, eating watermelon, pulling wagons
of hay all around me when he comes in with his black
photon gun and shoots me in the head, tells me I'm dead.
Soon enough, I mumble back, looking into his jaguar
mask, the eight fanged teeth ready to sink into my neck,
the ears slanted, the green eyes glaring.
What do you want, I snort, but he raises the gun
again, shoots me right in the open eye, says Die, Die,
and I remember the black wings one Sunday morning
landing on my father's chest to carry him off,
how he swung at them but missed, amazed finally
at the very air punching him back.
When I open my eyes my son is closing the door,
looking over his shoulder to be sure
I drop to the floor the way I am supposed
to, and I watch him test the handle, hear him
run down the steps because he knows already
how long his father will hold his breath,
how long I will lie here before rising
with the power of life and follow.

# Pennsylvania January

Our cat's got leukemia, the wood's
still wet for burning because I split
it late, and it's cold, below
zero with a wind down the hill. I
groan lifting the large logs
to the chopping block, set
the wedge and bring the twelve-pound maul
down to split the near-frozen oak, hearing now
my three-year-old tapping at the window,
as he likes to do, waving at me
when I turn around. And behind him, in
the red flannel shirt, his mother
smiling, pointing down as though
I might miss what our son does, making
her face, which is all tenderness and caring,
both of them waving and tapping until
I have to smile back, go to the cold
pane and smudge my nose and lips to theirs,
all three of us sliding our faces
and laughing in cold January.

Other Books of Poetry by MILKWEED EDITIONS

*Amen*
by Yehuda Amichai

*Civil Blood*
by Jill Breckenridge

*Windy Tuesday Nights*
Poems by Ralph Burns, Photographs by Roger Pfingston

*Eating the Sting*
by John Caddy

*The Man with Red Suspenders*
by Philip Dacey

*One Age in a Dream*
Diane Glancy

*Sacred Hearts*
by Phebe Hanson

*In a Sheep's Eye, Darling*
by Margaret Hasse

*Boxelder Bug Variations*
by Bill Holm

*How We Missed Belgium*
Poems in collaboration
by Deborah Keenan and Jim Moore

*Earth Tongues*
by Joe Paddock